Disney's
Family Storybook Library

Hard Work
Deserves Reward

Stories About Honesty and Integrity

BOOK THREE

Hard Work
Deserves Reward

Stories About Honesty and Integrity

Introduction

Doing what is right makes us feel good about ourselves. Sometimes, however, the temptations that surround us prove irresistible. Children are eager to please; to receive our smiles and encouragement; a pat on the back for a job well done. It's important to channel their exuberant energy into positive behavior. It's our responsibility to model the qualities and values we expect our children to internalize and follow.

Mickey and the cruel Queen both transgress. The Sorcerer's Apprentice is just beginning to understand the magical powers of the sorcerer. He needs to learn an important lesson about respect and humility. The evil Queen, who prizes her own beauty and vanity above all else, lacks integrity and pays the ultimate price for her selfish ways.

Mirror, Mirror on the Wall

from *Snow White and the Seven Dwarfs*

Jealousy of someone else's beauty
only makes you more unattractive.

Once upon a time, a very beautiful but cruel queen owned a magic mirror. Every time she looked into it, she asked the same thing:

"*Magic mirror on the wall,*
Who is the fairest one of all?"

The mirror always answered that she was the fairest in the land, until one day it replied:

"*Famed is thy beauty, Majesty.*
But hold—a lovely maid I see!
Alas she is more fair than thee!"

The vain
queen knew
at once that the
mirror spoke of
the Princess
Snow White.
The Queen
vowed that the
Princess must
die.

Using her
evil magic,
the Queen
transformed
herself into
an ugly old
beggar woman.
In her disguise,

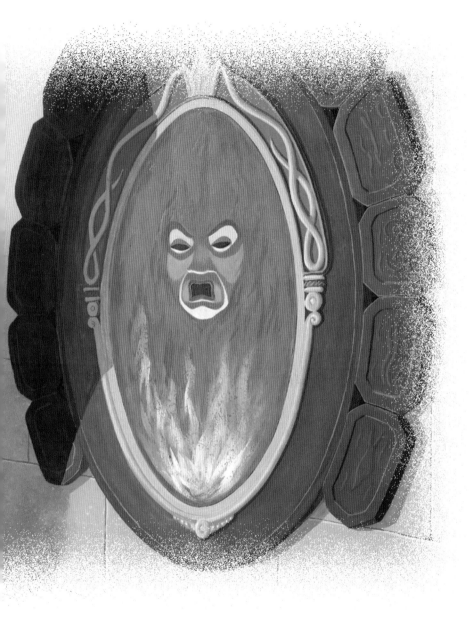

she went out to the forest where Snow White lived in hiding. Hanging on her arm was a basket of poisoned apples.

Snow White was not alone in the forest. She lived in the cottage of the seven dwarfs— Doc, Happy, Sleepy, Sneezy, Bashful, Grumpy, and Dopey. They loved her gentle goodness and vowed to protect her from the wicked queen. Each day, before they left to work in the diamond mine, they warned Snow White to be careful.

Snow White knew that the Queen wanted to harm her, but she had no idea that the beggar woman who came to the cottage was her enemy! She kindly invited her inside.

"Hello, dearie," croaked the old woman. "Would you like to try one of my delicious apples?"

The forest birds and animals tried to warn Snow White, but it was too late. She took a bite of an apple and fell down in a deep sleep.

"Now I am the fairest in the land!" shrieked the hag.

The animals raced through the woods to the diamond mine. The dwarfs hurried back to their cottage and chased the wicked queen up a mountain. Suddenly, a bolt of lightning struck the rock where the Queen stood, and she fell from the cliff, never to be seen again.

The dwarfs promised that they would never again leave Snow White's side. They stood guard beside her throughout the year, night and day, until one day, a young prince rode up.

The Prince recognized Snow White as the young woman he had once loved. Gently, he leaned over and kissed her. Snow White's eyes opened. The spell was broken at last! And they all lived happily ever after.

Mickey's Magical Mix-up

from *The Sorcerer's Apprentice*

⟨⟨⟨⟨

*It takes a lot of learning to control
a little magic—study hard.*

L ong ago, a powerful sorcerer agreed to
take on an apprentice.

Day in and day out, the sorcerer busied
himself with his spells and incantations while
Mickey did all the chores. As Mickey swept
the floors, tended the fire, and filled the
vat, he dreamed of becoming a sorcerer. He
knew he would make a fine magician, if only
the sorcerer would stop for a moment and
teach him a trick or two. The sorcerer had
promised!

Late one night, the sorcerer placed his

tall, pointed hat on the table and turned
toward the stairs that led to his bedchamber.
"When you've filled the vat with water from
the fountain, then you, too, may go to bed,"
said the sorcerer.

"Yes, sir," said Mickey, watching him climb

the stairs. Never before had the sorcerer forgotten his enchanted hat!

As soon as he was gone, Mickey ran over to the table and tried on the hat. Instantly Mickey felt that he, too, could make magic. The sorcerer need never find out.

Mickey spied an old straw broom in the corner. Using his newfound powers, he chanted, "Dooma, dooma, brooma, brooma."

The broom sprang to life. Mickey commanded the broom to lift two buckets and follow him to the fountain in the courtyard. The broom filled the buckets with water and marched back to the vat. As soon as the broom finished, Mickey motioned for it to fetch more water.

Quite satisfied, Mickey sat in a comfortable chair and fell asleep. Soon

he began to dream. Atop a pinnacle, surrounded by the sea, Mickey raised his arms to command the elements: fire, water, wind, and earth. Shooting stairs whirled around his head. The tides rose higher and higher until they splashed at his feet. He could almost feel the waves tickling his toes. . . .

Mickey awoke abruptly. He was sitting waist-high in water. All along, the broom had continued to fetch the water and fill the vat, and now the room was flooded.

"Stop! Halt!" Mickey cried, but the broom continued. He searched for the sorcerer's book of incantations, but it had disappeared.

In desperation, Mickey grabbed an axe and chopped the broom into pieces. To Mickey's horror, the splinters sprang

to life, each holding buckets. Blindly they
marched to the fountain and back, filling
the vat with water.

The room became a turbulent sea. When the missing book of incantations drifted by, Mickey climbed aboard. Frantically he turned the pages, trying to find a spell that would stop the brooms.

Suddenly the sorcerer threw open the door and murmured the incantation. The waters receded, and Mickey sat, shamefaced, in a puddle. As the sorcerer glared at him,

Mickey vowed that he would never make
magic again . . . that is, until the sorcerer
felt he was ready!